PRAISE FOR BAD PANDA

WINNE

North Somerset Teach

Surrey Libraries Children's Book Award

Fantastic Book Awards

SHORTLISTED

Sainsbury's Children's Book Awards

Alligator's Mouth Award

Leicester Libraries Best Book Award

Sheffield Children's Book Award

Crystal Kite Award

'**Hilarious!** Wonderfully warm illustrations.'

Sarah McIntyre

'Silliness aplenty in this **uproarious** beginning to a potentially addictive new series.'

Guardian

'Every page is **packed with laughs**.'

Michelle Robinson

'Full of laughs.'

Tom Fletcher

'Hilarity bordering on **genius**.'

Dapo Adeola

'**Super-readable** as well as super-fun.'

LoveReading4Kids

'S**uper-funny and super-silly**.'
Lancashire Post

'Children will undoubtedly **love** this.'
The Bookbag

'Misunderstandings, slapstick and giant poo . . .
what more could a young reader want?'
Kirkus

'**Perfect** for fans of Pamela Butchart and Alex T. Smith.'
Book Lover Jo

'This book is just funny . . . **sure to be a hit**.'
INIS Magazine

'Side-splittingly witty.'
Echo Live

'**Delightfully funny** (and a bit rude!).'
Irish Independent

'An **amusing** tale with lively illustrations.'
Sunday Express

'**Hilarious** . . . perfect for newly confident readers.'
Mini Travellers

'**Readers will love it** as it is full of daring and
bravery, and much backfiring of
ridiculous schemes.'
School Librarian

FABER has published children's books since 1929. T. S. Eliot's *Old Possum's Book of Practical Cats* and Ted Hughes' *The Iron Man* were amongst the first. Our catalogue at the time said that 'it is by reading such books that children learn the difference between the shoddy and the genuine'. We still believe in the power of reading to transform children's lives. All our books are chosen with the express intention of growing a love of reading, a thirst for knowledge and to cultivate empathy. We pride ourselves on responsible editing. Last but not least, we believe in kind and inclusive books in which all children feel represented and important.

SWAPNA HADDOW is the award-winning author of the Dave Pigeon and Bad Panda series. She lives in New Zealand with her husband, son and their dog, Archie.

ALSO BY SWAPNA HADDOW

Bad Panda

Bad Panda: The Cake Escape

Dave Pigeon

Dave Pigeon (Nuggets!)

Dave Pigeon (Racer!)

Dave Pigeon (Royal Coo!)

Dave Pigeon (Kittens!)

Mites, Camera, Action!

Swapna Haddow

faber

First published in the UK in 2024
First published in the US in 2024
by Faber and Faber Limited
The Bindery, 51 Hatton Garden
London, EC1N 8HN
faber.co.uk

Typeset in Sweater School by Faber
This font has been specially chosen to support reading

Printed in India

Illustrations by Dynamo Ltd in the style of Sheena Dempsey
with express permission

A CIP record for this book is available from the British Library

ISBN 978–0–571–37927–9

Printed and bound on FSC® paper in line with our continuing commitment to ethical business practices, sustainability and the environment. For further information see faber.co.uk/environmental-policy

2 4 6 8 10 9 7 5 3 1

For Haddow Class at Horndean CE Junior School – you are all superstars!

S. H.

1
The Lin Show

'Lin,' Liony McLion-Face whispered into the fluffy ear of the sleeping panda. 'Are you awake?'

Lin, who was very much awake but wanting to lie in, stayed as still as possible.

'Liii-iiin,' the lion crooned again. 'Wakey-wakey.'

Lin held her breath, hoping the lion might think she was dead and leave her alone.

'Lin, Lin, Lin, Lin, Lin, Lin, Lin, Lin, Lin, Lin, Lin, Lin, Lin, Lin, Lin, Lin, Lin, Lin, Lin, Lin, Lin, Lin, Lin, Lin, Lin, Lin, Lin, Lin, Lin, Lin, Lin, Lin, Lin, Lin, Lin, Lin, Lin, Lin, Lin, Lin Lin Lin Lin Lin Lin Lin Lin Lin Lin Lin Lin Lin Lin Lin Lin Lin Lin, Lin, LinLinLinLinLinLinLinLinLinLinLinLinLinLinLinLin LinLinLin, LIN LIN LIN LIN!'

'What?' Lin snapped.

'Oh good, you're up,' Liony said. 'I hope

I didn't wake you.'

Lin growled and rolled over in her hammock. She rubbed her eyes with her paws and allowed the morning light in.

'What's that noise?' she asked, sitting up.

Instead of the usual morning din of the zoo's dawn chorus and the rhythmic whacking of balls on bats as the tigers played table tennis with the penguins, there was another sound in its place. The grind of wheels on tarmac and the grumbles and mumbles of humans pulsated loudly against Lin's eardrums.

It was a sound Lin had become somewhat familiar with since moving to the zoo. She had noticed that humans made many unusual sounds. When they were happy, instead of just growling like normal animals, they made a tinkly tittering sound. And when they were angry, instead of just growling like normal animals, they made a loud honking sound. And when they wanted an ice cream, instead of just growling like normal animals, they made a 'I think it's time for an ice cream, don't you, dear?' sort of sound.

Lin had decided that humans were indeed the strangest of the strange . . . and she had met an actual sparklemuffin spider.

'Lin,' Liony squealed. 'I have delightful news: we are going to be famous!'

Fu, Lin's best friend and paddock mate, sat up in his hammock. He cleared the sleep from his eyes and peered at Liony. 'Famous?' he asked.

'That's right, my little panda pompoms! We are being filmed for a documentary,' the lion replied, flipping his golden mane over his shoulder. 'We're going to be stars.'

Fu tumbled out of his hammock and landed in a heap on the grassy tussock below. 'Lin! We are going to be movie stars!'

Lin yawned. She couldn't have been less bothered about the news. She was about as

bothered about the news as your neighbour's dog's cousin would be about the crumpled yoghurt lid from your packed lunch sitting at the bottom of your schoolbag. Lin was officially the most famous panda in the world, and she was officially totally over fame.

But Liony refused to let Lin put a downer on his joyous day. He pinged the corner of Lin's hammock, sending her toppling out onto Fu. He then dusted off the two bears and drew them close as he pointed to a human in the distance.

Lin watched as people ran around the human, sprucing his hair and fluffing his jumper. He seemed to her to be the most important of the human herd.

'That's Avid Dattenburrow,' Liony said. 'He makes those animal documentaries that you see posters for all over the zoo.'

'I've seen those posters!' Fu exclaimed. 'I don't like that one with the bobbit worm.'

Liony grimaced. 'I remember that poster. I think one of the penguins drew a moustache and a top hat on it.'

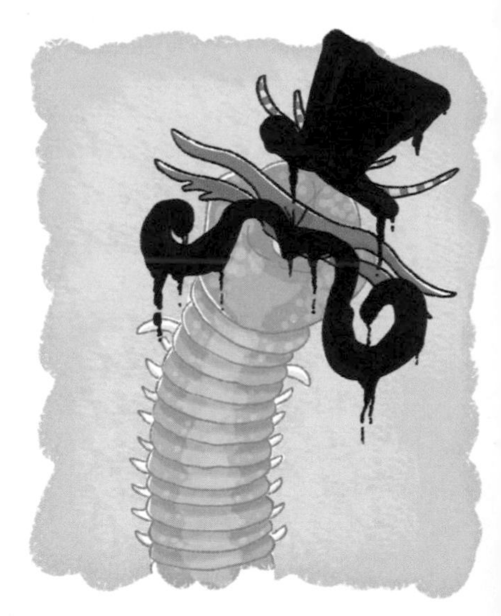

As Liony and Fu discussed bobbit worms and whether top hats made them look more or less sinister, Lin sensed her chance to slip away from the lion and clamber back into her hammock for a late-morning snooze.

'You know, these animal movies are watched around the world by everyone,' Liony continued, knowledgeably.

The fur on Lin's back prickled and she stopped mid-climb. 'Everyone?' she asked.

'**Everyone**,' Liony confirmed with a smug smile.

'Well, that's exciting, isn't it?' Fu whistled.

Lin spun on her heel and rejoined Liony and Fu. She observed Avid Dattenburrow as he moved among the swarm of humans towards a camera. He stopped to clear a way for a row of ants as they marched towards a sugar lump.

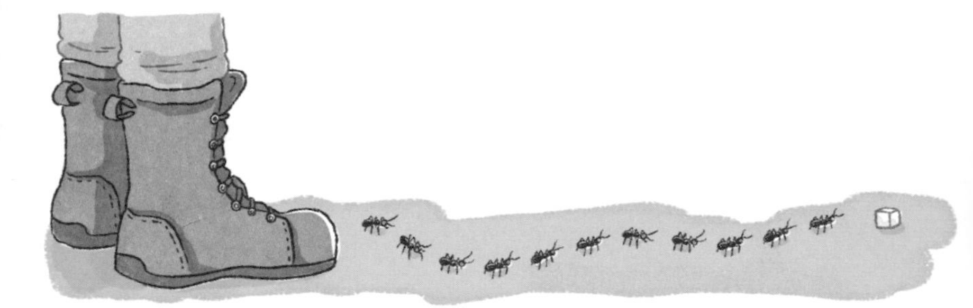

Normally, Lin would be wary of humans. They

smelled like a mix of gone-off bamboo and Fu's feet after two weeks of not washing. They ate their food out of packets and off plates whereas Lin liked to eat straight off the ground or out of Fu's ears. And, most importantly, humans didn't seem to have much in common with pandas at all. Humans loved doing maths and pandas didn't really have a clue what maths was.

Nope. They didn't have a single thing in common.

And yet . . .

While Lin had settled in at the zoo and found a family of sorts, she still missed her beloved big brother back at home at the panda sanctuary something rotten. She had been desperate to get a message home to Face-Like-A-Bag-Of-Potatoes ever since she'd arrived there. Now it seemed that there was finally a way to do it.

'Let's make a movie!' Lin grinned at Liony and Fu.

2
Still Very Much The Lin Show

Liony pranced off towards the hippos to spread the movie news.

'I don't think we should have let Liony go,' Lin said, wringing her paws.

'It's quite hard to hold on to a lion,' Fu said. 'They can be a bit bitey and clawy when they want to be.'

‘Why do you want to keep Liony here?’ Fu asked. ‘You’re usually annoyed by how much of our nap time he wastes with his chitter-chatter.’

‘I don’t think it’s a good idea if Liony tells everyone about the documentary,’ Lin said.

‘Why not?’ Fu questioned. ‘We’re all going to be movie stars!’

‘Shhh,’ Lin hushed. ‘I don’t want everyone to know.’

Fu scratched his head. And then his bottom. And then his head again. ‘I’m pretty sure everyone knows, Lin. Those humans are making a right old racket with their cameras,' he said. He pointed in the direction of the hippos. 'And besides, Liony is spreading the word quickly.'

'I know.' Lin frowned. 'It's very annoying, because I really don't need everyone else hogging the camera.'

Fu smirked. For as long as he had known Lin, she'd always wanted to downplay her fame. Now there was a chance for everyone to get the movie-star treatment, she was ready to panda-kick the lot of them out of the spotlight.

'Well, well, Lin,' Fu joked. 'It turns out you **do** love being a bit of a celebrity after all.'

'Don't be ridiculous,' Lin huffed. 'Of course I don't.'

'So why don't you want the others in the documentary?'

'Think about it, Fu,' Lin growled, stomping her feet.

So he did.

I need to use this documentary . . .
To launch a new haircare range for pandas?
No!
As a platform to talk about the plight of unicorns?
No! Anyway, what's up with unicorns?
Have you seen any around?
No...
Exactly. It's because something is up.

Lin sighed. As much as she loved her best friend, they were rarely on the same page. Like the time she'd hinted she would like a bamboo smoothie for breakfast and Fu made her a new swing set out of long stems and a bin lid. And the time she'd hinted she wanted a nap and he'd invited over all the kākāpō for a birdy dance off. And the time, well basically just all the time, every time.

'Fu, this is my chance to get a message home to my brother!' Lin said.

'Of course!' Fu cheered. And then he did the confused scratching thing again, moving from his head to his butt and back to his head again. 'How?'

'With the movie!'

Fu stared blankly at Lin.

'I record a message on camera.'

Fu stared even more blankly at Lin.

'And everyone around the world will watch the movie.'

Fu stared so blankly at Lin that she was ninety-seven per cent sure he had fallen asleep standing up with his eyes wide open.

'And Face-Like-A-Bag-Of-Potatoes will see the movie and he'll know I'm OK!'

A wide smile broke across Fu's fuzzy face. 'That's a great idea, Lin! I wish I'd thought of it.'

'**Now** can you understand why I can't have everyone else in this movie?' Lin said. 'I can't have them wasting a single precious minute of the film when I need to let Face-Like-A-Bag-Of-Potatoes know where I am and how I'm doing.' Lin's forehead furrowed with concern. 'He'll be worried about me.'

(At that exact moment in time, Face-Like-A-Bag-Of-Potatoes was fast

asleep, dreaming about

race-car washing machines and flying tacos. But when he eventually wakes up, does his morning poo, has his breakfast, does his second morning poo, he will, of course, think about his little sister Lin for a moment before going back to thinking about flying tacos.)

'It's very important that you help me make sure this movie stays on course,' Lin told Fu.

Fu saluted his best friend, ready to help.

'Right, let's find that Avid Dattenburrow!' Lin ordered, marching towards the zoo gift shop.

3

The Lin Show Featuring That Guy off the Nature Documentaries

'I am Avid Dattenburrow and I've been lucky enough to spend my life exploring the wild places of our planet,' said Avid Dattenburrow, looking into the camera lens. His lullaby-gentle tone could have soothed a riotous stampede of wildebeest to sleep. He continued, 'I've travelled all over the globe and I can honestly say I have never seen a zoo quite like this.'

'And CUT!' a woman by the camera shouted.

Lin and Fu stayed crouched behind the ice-cream freezer as they watched the humans gather around the one they called 'Avid Dattenburrow'.

He was a round man with a short white mane that flapped over his head. He reminded Lin of

a panda elder she once knew who had lived a life as a rock star and now spent his retirement sharing stories of his past with young panda musicians and handing out sticky bamboo sweeties to panda cubs just before their dinner. Yes, Avid Dattenburrow was **that** panda. He had a smell that said a monkey would sit, content, on his shoulders, swatting flies off his silver tresses – it was a smell that Lin rather liked.

'That's great, Avid,' the woman by the camera yelled. 'Now let's get some footage of the animals roaming free in the zoo.'

As the crew of humans funnelled towards the front of the zoo where the lions wandered, Avid hung back.

He'd spotted two sets of fluffy black ears poking out from behind the ice-cream freezer and was reminded of the excitement he felt as a young man when he first started filming his nature documentaries.

'Lin?' Fu whispered. 'I think that Avid Dattenburrow is coming over.'

'Good,' Lin said. 'We'll capture him and use him as a hostage to make sure our demands are met.'

'What demands?' Fu asked.

'That we get to use the movie to send a message to Face-Like-A-Bag-Of-Potatoes! Keep up, Fu!' Lin tutted at her friend. 'These humans are a tricky sort of animal. They are rude, they think they own the planet, they wear shoes, and they have no respect for personal space. We have to be on our guard.'

'Hello there,' came a gentle voice from across the other side of the ice-cream freezer.

Lin popped up just enough to spot the white mane of Avid Dattenburrow.

'It's OK,' Avid reassured them. 'I have bamboo cake for you.'

He slid his hand midway across the freezer and placed two bamboo cakes carefully on top,

making sure not to come any closer than he already had.

'Are you sure they are a tricky sort of animal?' Fu asked. 'He brought us cake.'

Lin eyed the old man with suspicion, but she reached across anyway and took the cake because she was brought up to always eat cake.

'I think he has very kind eyes,' Fu said, chomping his cake and studying the man in front of them.

'They're a bit close together, if you ask me,' Lin growled, though she had to admit the cake was exceptional and this Avid Dattenburrow creature was being very respectful of her personal space.

The man reached into his pocket and pulled out more cake. He tore it in half and slid it towards Lin and Fu. Only this time he kept his arm stretched across the freezer.

'Should we shake his paw?' Fu asked.

Lin had never been offered a paw in such a way from a human, but instinct told her to reach across and offer hers.

As their paws touched, Lin's gaze met Avid's and a tenderness descended upon them both. In that instant it was as though they somehow

knew what it was like to walk a mile in each other's paws. This was the first time Lin had ever felt a mutual respect for a human and she had to admit she quite liked the warm feeling growing in her chest.

'Are we still taking him hostage?' Fu asked.

'I'm not sure,' Lin replied, pulling back from the man.

'I really want to hug him. Can I hug him?'

'No! You can't hug a potential hostage.'

Before either of them could decide whether to hug or kidnap the TV presenter, the loud woman by the camera returned. 'We're going to have to stop filming, Avid,' she barked. 'We have a HUGE problem.'

4
The Lin Show is CANCELLED!

'WHAT?' Avid, Lin and Fu said at the same time, although it sounded more like a bunch of bear growls and a human saying 'what'.

'Here,' the woman sighed, tugging a screen

out of her bag. 'It's a disaster.'

Avid watched the screen while Lin and Fu peered over his shoulder.

'What's the problem?' they all asked at the same time. Again it sounded like a bunch of bear growls and a human saying 'what's the problem?'.

'It's BORING!' the woman said.

'It's real life,' Avid replied.

'No one wants to watch a bunch of animals sleeping and eating and scratching their bums all day long!' the woman cried.

'But that's exactly what animals do all day,' Avid argued.

'He's not wrong,' Fu said.

'I don't scratch my bum all day long,' Lin retorted.

'I do,' Fu replied with a little smile.

'Our viewers want to see action!' the woman said, waving her hands wildly. 'They want to see baby flamingos stuck in sand on the verge of death and orcas whacking herrings in the face and weird worms that pop up from the ocean floor and give you nightmares for days.' She slapped the back of her hand on the screen. 'There's no drama here.'

Fu giggled. 'Liony is going to be furious that she didn't find him dramatic enough.'

'Fu! This is no time to laugh at Liony,' Lin cried. 'That's for the end of the day.' She pulled Fu close as the humans continued to argue. '**This** is a disaster.'

'Why?' Fu asked.

'Because if they decide we're too boring, they won't film us and I won't get to send my message home. I can't let those boring penguins be the reason I can't get a video to Face-Like-A-Bag-Of-Potatoes!'

Avid seemed to sense the pandas knew what was going on. He smiled apologetically as though he was embarrassed not only about the woman's rant about boring animals, but also because it seemed that the entire human race wouldn't be happy just to watch a show about a couple of pandas sitting around scratching their bottoms.

Lin felt a warm feeling in her chest again as she met Avid's gaze and she had the overwhelming urge to hum a happy tune that sounded a bit like this:

Hmmmm, hmmmm, hmm, hmmm, hmmmmmm, hmmmmm, hmmmmmm, hmmmmmm, hmmmmm, hmmmmm, hmm, hmm, hmmm (you know the one – join in) *hmmmm, hmmm, hm, hmmmmmm,*

hmmmmmm, ahhhhhh,

AHHHHHHH!

Instead of humming, Lin attempted to smile back . . . but having never returned a human smile before, she made a face that looked a lot like she'd just stepped on a hedgehog.

'I don't want to give up on this zoo just yet,' Avid told the camerawoman. 'I **know** there's a story here. I just need to find it.'

The woman sighed again and rubbed the

sides of her head. 'I suppose it's too late to find another location for filming.' She wagged her finger at Avid, her face tight. 'You have the next hour to find a story. Otherwise I'm bringing in the **animal actors**.'

'Don't worry. I'll find a story,' Avid said, reassuring the woman who was already walking away.

He turned to Lin and Fu. 'And you two are going to help me find it.'

5

The ~~Lin~~ Liony Show

Just like all pandas would've done in that situation, Lin and Fu completely misunderstood Avid's request to team up, and crawled off in the opposite direction, leaving the TV presenter alone to scratch his head in confusion.

'What's an animal actor?' Lin said as the pandas rounded the corner of the central fountain, where the penguins and pigeons were mastering their backstroke.

'No idea,' Fu replied as they took the path down towards the main gate. 'But I heard a good joke about an actor once. Do you want to hear it?'

'No,' Lin said.

Why do you say 'break a leg' to an actor?
Because every actor needs a plaster.
I want no part of this joke.
Are you sure that's not meant to be 'every actor needs a cast'?
Why would that be funny?

'Lin!' Liony galloped towards them. 'We have a problem!'

'Why are **his** problems always a **we** problem?' Lin muttered to Fu, slowing down nonetheless to let the lion catch up with them.

'I don't think he has a wee problem, Lin,' Fu replied. 'It's just a little dribble every now and then, and I think that's what happens when you get older.'

'A **we** problem, Fu,' Lin cried, gesturing to the both of them. 'Not a **wee** problem!'

‘Do you have a wee problem, Lin?’ Liony asked, hearing the end of the pandas’ conversation. ‘Because it’s nothing to be ashamed of. We all get caught out once in a while.’

‘NO!’ Lin roared. ‘I do not have a WEE PROBLEM.’

For a moment, the whole zoo was completely silent. The most silent any silent place has ever been. Like a loud supermarket going absolutely dead quiet just at the moment you think it’s safe to let out a really loud trumpet fart.

She definitely has a wee problem.

You can tell by the way she waddles.

I thought that's just how all pandas walk.

Maybe they all have wee problems.

'What's wrong, Liony?' Lin sighed, aware that the penguins were eyeing her in a judgemental way.

'**They've** arrived,' Liony said, pointing a sharp claw towards the front of the zoo.

Lin couldn't quite make out what Liony was pointing at. She clambered on top of Fu to get a better view.

'Who are **they**?' she said, squinting to see.

'That's my cousin Singa,' Liony seethed. 'And his herd of actors.'

'Actors?' Fu managed to squeak as Lin trod

on his snout.

'They're the animal actors. And they are professionals. They've been professionally trained by humans at RADA to play roles on TV and the big screen,' Lion replied.

'RADA?' Lin questioned.

'The Royal Academy of Dramatic Animals,' Liony answered. 'Of course, I could've been a star too but Singa was so desperate to be an actor, I gave up my place at drama school for him.' Liony flicked back his mane and inspected his claws as though he wasn't bothered by his superstar cousin in the slightest. 'I didn't want to tread on Singa's paws, you see.'

'Why are they here?' Lin asked.

'I'm pretty sure they are here to steal **our** show,' Liony ranted.

'So you're not certain?' Lin said.

'I'm pretty certain.'

'So you're definitely certain?'

'I'm as certain as certain can be without being certain.'

‘How certain is that?!’ Lin said, exasperated.

‘Pretty certain,’ Liony retorted.

‘Gah,’ Lin groaned. ‘I’m going to find out for certain.’

She rolled off Fu’s shoulders and stalked over to the group of animals gathered by the black trailer marked ‘ANIMAL ACTORS’ in gold curvy writing.

As she got closer, she noticed each animal had a human of their own who was pruning their fur and brushing their manes. There was a second human for each animal too, polishing their nails and massaging their paws.

Lin, who had spent her whole life wishing she wasn't so cute, suddenly felt very conscious of the panda-cake crumbs wedged in her chin fur and the bedhead ears she hadn't yet groomed that morning.

She rubbed down her fur and stood tall, plumping up her ears and hoping she looked her best.

She spotted Singa immediately. He was an

identical version of Liony but shinier. His mane was more lustrous, and his golden fur glittered as he sunned his face in the late-morning light.

'Hello,' Lin said as she sidled over to the lion.

'If you want an autograph, please leave your name with the lemur at my trailer,' Singa said, not even turning his head one degree to try and make eye contact with Lin.

Lin glanced over at a busy lemur who was scurrying between the animal actors and replacing cucumbers over their eyes.

'I'm not here for an autograph,' Lin said.

Singa tipped his chin and stared down his nose at Lin.

'I don't owe you money, do I?' Singa said. He cocked his head to one side. 'Oh no. We're not **related**, are we?'

'No,' Lin said. 'We are definitely not related.'

'Thank goodness,' the lion chuckled. 'That would've been hard to explain to the gang at drama school—'

'But I know someone who **is** related to

you,' Lin interrupted. 'I'm friends with Liony McLion-Face.'

Singa almost fell out of his chair.

'Gosh! That's a blast from the past. How is the old fella?' Singa asked. He looked around, as though he had just noticed he was in a zoo for the first time. 'So this is where he wound up then? I don't suppose he's nearby, is he?'

'Yes, he's right over there . . .' Lin said. She turned to point at Liony, who she thought was behind her, and paused when all she could see was Fu with a huge lion trying to hide behind him.

'He's behind the panda,' she sighed, waving at Fu to step aside.

'Liony!' Singa crooned.

'Singa,' Liony muttered back.

'What are you doing over there? Come here and give your cousin a hug!' Singa laughed.

Before Liony could move, Singa leaped forward and caught Liony in a headlock. They tussled as Liony tried to push him away but Singa kept a tight grip.

'Get. Off. Of. Me,' Liony said through gritted teeth.

'I'm just playing,' Singa chuckled. He turned to Lin and Fu. 'He's always so serious.'

'No, he's not,' Fu said, defending his friend.

'Yesterday we spent thirty minutes laughing at a stick that looked like a twig. It was very funny.'

An awkward silence fell over the group. And then Fu laughed, remembering the stick-twig thing and made it even more awkward.

Lin thought about how much she missed her big brother. She imagined him walking through the gates of the zoo, a pile of bamboo stems under his arm. They'd roll at speed to one another before giving each other the biggest hug.

Looking at Singa wrestling poor Liony to the ground made Lin's blood boil. She would give anything to see her family again and here was Singa bullying his cousin. But Lin didn't want to embarrass her friend, so she swallowed down the heat rising up from her chest, unclenched her fists and took a slow breath.

She cleared her throat. 'Sorry to ask, Singa, but what are you doing here in our zoo?'

The lion dropped his cousin and stared at Lin.

'I'm going to be in a movie about the zoo, of course,' he answered.

'So there are going to be two movies?' Fu asked, helping Liony up off the pavement.

'Oh no,' Singa crooned. 'Only **one**.' He leaned in close and spoke in hushed tones. 'Apparently the animals here are soooo boring, they had to get us professionals in to liven things up. We're here to replace those amateurs.'

Liony glared at his cousin. 'We are not amateurs.'

'Oh,' Singa said in mock embarrassment, his paw flying up to cover his mouth. 'I had no idea **you** were the boring animals they were talking about. I wouldn't have said anything if I knew.'

'We are not boring!' Lin said, balling up her fists.

'If you say so,' the lion laughed.

Lin bared her teeth at the lion, her nostrils flared and her eyes fixed hard on his. She stepped back and kicked a nearby bin, sending ice-cream wrappers and paper cups tornadoing down the pristine path.

'Now, now,' Singa mocked. 'No need to be such a **bad panda**.'

He smirked at the trio and sauntered off back to his pampering session just as Liony grabbed Lin, restraining her from charging at the retreating lion.

'You were right, Liony,' Fu said. 'They **are** here to steal our show.'

'No,' Lin growled, interrupting Fu. 'I won't let them.' The veins in her face strained against her skin with rage (though you couldn't see them because of her massive fluff-ball head). The last time she had been called a 'bad panda', she'd felt a rage so powerful, like a thousand charging buffalo, surge though her body. When Lin was a 'bad panda' there was no reasoning with the angry bear – she was ready to be her naughtiest.

Lin turned to Fu and Liony. 'We are going to steal our film back!' she roared, her eyes flashing full of bad pandaness.

6
The Lin Show will NOT be Cancelled

'Are we going to cuddle that cuddly human?' Fu asked hopefully.

Fu and Liony trotted at speed alongside Lin, who was storming towards the crew of humans.

'We are not cuddling anyone!' Lin barked. 'We are taking back our show from Singa and his herd.'

'But how?' Liony panted. Pandas were surprisingly fast when they were on a mission. 'The animal actors are **professionals**.'

Lin stopped so suddenly that Fu and Liony almost barrelled into each other and over a bench to stop from colliding with her.

'We are **all** professionals! How can you have professional animals? Animals are animals and we are animals too!' Lin cried. She stomped her paw down and pointed at the camera crew who had gathered by the gift shop. 'These humans have come here to film our zoo. OUR zoo.' Lin jabbed a paw at her chest. 'I will not let some drama-school lion steal a show about us **from** us. This is my one chance to get a message home to my brother.'

'Good for you, Lin!' Liony cheered, slapping his paws together in agreement. 'How can we help?'

'I want that Avid Dattenburrow. I have a feeling he's on our side and he can help us,' Lin declared.

'I'll get the bird crew on it,' Liony said, saluting Lin and sprinting off towards the aviary.

'Fu, we need to make sure those humans do not start filming Singa and his friends. You and I have to show them we can be professional animals too.'

Fu high-pawed Lin and they headed straight for the camera crew.

'I found Avid Dattenburrow,' Liony roared as he joined the pandas.

Liony had not only found the elderly TV presenter, he'd decided to carry the human over to Lin and Fu like a mama lion would carry her baby.

'Put him down!' Lin commanded. 'He looks like he's about to faint. He probably thinks you are going to eat him!'

Liony plopped the old man on the floor. 'Eat him?' He shook his head in disgust. 'I'm actually thinking of becoming a vegetarian.'

'Oh really?' Fu said, interested. 'That's a great idea. It's much better for the planet.'

'I was thinking that,' Liony replied. 'But will it disrupt the natural order of things?'

'You two are getting distracted!' Lin said,

clapping her paws together. 'Help me out before Avid Dattenburrow runs off.'

Liony and Fu hadn't noticed the presenter backing away from them as he examined the lion-shaped tooth marks in his jacket where Liony had held on to him.

'Sorry about that,' Liony roared, shooting him his biggest smile.

Avid took a slow step back with his hands held high.

'More teeth, Liony,' Lin demanded. 'You know

your smile is your best feature. It'll reassure him that we are on the same side.'

'Good idea,' Liony said. 'Perhaps I'll show him my back teeth now I've finally managed to get last week's corn cob unstuck.'

Liony stalked up close to Avid and shot him his biggest, toothiest grin and then opened wide for good measure.

Avid's ragged, terrified breaths came out in short bursts as he inched even further away from the animals.

'Good work, Liony,' Lin commended. 'I think he's got the message.'

Lin held up her paws to match Avid's and spoke slowly to him. 'We need your help.'

Avid finally managed to tear his gaze from Liony's sharp teeth and focused on the pandas. He then took a moment to regard the trio of animals. What could possibly bring a couple of bears and a lion together, he pondered as Lin continued to roar at him in panda.

Slowly his confused look started to fade as his eyes widened. A flash of recognition crossed his face. 'I think you're trying to tell me something,' he murmured.

'We want to tell you something,' Lin said, hoping he understood her. 'We would like you to tell **our** story.'

'Are you trying to tell me you have a story to tell?' Avid said out loud to himself as he attempted to grasp what Lin was communicating.

'This is hopeless,' Lin said, throwing her paws up. 'He's never going to understand me.'

'He might understand this,' Fu said.

He threw a paw around Lin and a paw around Liony and hugged them close.

'What are you doing?' Lin said, struggling against the fluffy cuddle. She stopped as she spotted Avid's expression change.

A wide smile had stretched across the old man's face. He wrapped his own arms around himself, imitating the animals. 'I think I have my story,' he declared to the trio. 'It's a story about **your** family.'

7
Lin Takes Control of The Lin Show

'It's the best nature documentary I've ever seen,' Liony said, throwing a pawful of yesterday's cafe popcorn in his open jaw.

Unblinking, Lin, Fu and Liony watched Avid Dattenburrow and the camerawoman. There were no more smiles. Instead, hands were flapping, throats were being cleared louder and louder, and there was a lot of pacing. The humans' wild gestures and loud growls suggested to Lin that Avid was perhaps losing his battle to convince the woman that they should stick with the original zoo animals.

'This is not going well,' Lin said.

'I'm sure he just needs more time to convince

them,' Fu encouraged.

'We don't have time,' Liony said.

Lin followed Liony's gaze. The animal actors were leaving their pamper stations and prancing down the main path of the zoo towards the raccoons' leafy paddocks.

'Right,' Lin said. 'Let's grab the cameras and just do this ourselves, Fu!'

Lin thundered off towards a tent full of video cameras that had been set up near the cafe.

'What are we going to do with the cameras?'

Fu asked, hurrying to keep up with Lin.

'Film, of course!' Lin shouted over her shoulder.

She tore open the tent door, kicking over the pegs that held it in place.

The grey-green crinkly fabric rustled as Lin stormed in. Steel racks and huge black trunks lined the inside of the tent, keeping the shelter from toppling as Fu squeezed in after Lin.

It took a moment for the pandas' eyes to adjust to the dark. And when they did, Lin still had to rub her eyes to make sure what she was seeing was actually true.

'Hold on,' Lin cried, aghast. 'It's empty.'

Sure enough, there wasn't a single piece of equipment in sight. The racks had been cleared of cameras, cables and lights. Even the juice bottle on the table in the corner had been drunk dry.

Lin ducked out of the tent and looked around. Absolutely every single camera had disappeared.

'What's going on?' she exclaimed to the equally baffled Fu.

And that's when she spotted a shadow moving across the stone paving. Peering closer, she saw it was in fact a thick black cable, slithering away. A thick black cable that looked awfully similar to the ones needed for the video cameras.

'The ants!' she yelled. 'Follow that cable, Fu!'

A long row of tiny black ants marched onwards to the command of 'left, right, left, right' as they transported the cable mounted on their backs towards the ant hills.

And ahead of the cable was a camera, a microphone and a key light headed in the same direction.

Lin and Fu gave chase. Their fluffy legs pumped hard as they tried to match the speed of the ants. But the trail of insects snaked on further and further ahead.

'Oi, ants!' Lin shouted. 'Where do you think you're going?'

She paused, out of breath, as Fu went on. The ants were ridiculously fast despite their teeny-tiny legs. Normally this would have entertained the pandas. Nothing made Lin laugh more than fast, teeny-tiny legs. But as Lin struggled to keep up she felt dizzy, as though the air was being strangled out of her chest. She was panicking – the ants were disappearing with the cameras **she** needed.

'Wait!' Lin shouted, but the trail of camera equipment moved forward at pace. She threw her entire body at the line of ants, hoping to catch a wire or a cable, but instead she hit the ground hard as the ants scurried on.

Clutching her bruised paw, she sat slumped on the ground where she had landed, watching the only chance she had to send a message home disappear into an anthill.

'Ow!' Lin cried as a new sharp pain pinched her leg.

She scratched her fur and pulled up a little red mite on the edge of her claw that still had a tuft of panda fur in its jaws.

'What do you think you're doing?' Lin shrieked.

'What do you think **you're** doing?' the spider-shaped mite shouted back.

Lin couldn't make out what his little voice had said but just as she was about to squish him between her nails, a loudhailer crawled back down the line of ants towards her.

She picked it up in confusion and the mite on her nail crawled into the speaker.

'I said, what do you think **you** are doing?' the mite yelled into the microphone, just loud enough for Lin to hear.

'I need the camera!' she retorted.

A tiny cone travelled up her leg atop a black ant. The mite grabbed the cone, cupped his front legs around one of the open ends and shouted into the mic again.

'So do we,' he squared up, this time louder and clearer.

'Well, I'm bigger than you,' Lin shrugged.

'Well, I'm bitier than you,' the mite said, ready to chow down on Lin's paw again. 'The camera is mine or I set my troops on you.'

He snapped hard into the fluffy flesh on Lin's paw.

'OW! You bit me again!' Lin yelped.

A troop of one hundred ants filed up Lin's leg, across her back and followed the red mite up to her shoulder. Lin tried to shake them off as another hundred ants joined the troop, clinging to her fur. Soon her entire back was covered in a swarm of tiny ants, burrowing deep into her skin.

And that was the last thing Lin remembered as she stumbled back in pain and crumpled to the ground under the sting of one thousand and one ant bites.

8

No One Knows Whose Show It Is Any More . . .

Dazed and groggy, Lin grimaced as the sharp pain of the bite stung. She tried to reach a paw to rub the sore spot, but she could not wrestle her legs free.

'What's going on?'

She twisted as much as she could and saw that she was being carted into a large anthill by hundreds of thousands of ants.

'Put me down!' she yelled.

The ants jumped aside on command and in formation, dropping Lin hard on her bottom.

Lin jolted up. The floor was made of grit and dirt and made her fur itch. Her head knocked against the clay walls, causing a tiny avalanche of twigs and sand to waterfall down her back.

She blinked to let her eyes get used to the dark cave. There were millions of mites glaring up at her and her bruised bottom began to ache. But she forgot about the pain as soon as she spotted Fu trembling in the corner while a parade of ants cinched his paws tight with camera cables.

'Let him go!' she growled.

As she moved to stand up, her bound legs collapsed beneath her.

'What's going on?' she demanded again,

falling back on to her bottom.

'You are my hostages,' came a voice from beyond Fu.

'What?' Fu cried.

'Hostages,' the voice yelled again.

'Did you say sausages?' Fu wailed. 'Pandas do not make good sausages.'

'Hostages! I said HOSTAGES!'

'But pigs are much better at being sausages,' Fu whimpered. 'And cows. And chickens. And vegetables. And maybe even some rocks . . .'

'You should probably turn the volume up on that thing if you want Fu to stop crying,' Lin interrupted. 'I also heard sausages.'

There was a nod of agreement from the ants by Lin's paws.

'Fine,' the voice said. 'IS THIS BETTER?'

'Much better,' Lin said.

The loudhailer moved towards Lin, carried by the ants, and Lin noticed that the same tiny red mite who had bitten her earlier was now standing tall upon a pyramid of ants and speaking into the microphone again.

'Let's try this again,' the red mite yelled. 'I am the chief lieutenANT and you are my hostages!'

'Let us go,' Lin barked.

'Not until you promise to leave the cameras with us,' the lieutenant replied.

'No!' Lin said. She wrestled with the ties on her paws, scratching and gnawing but unable to break free. 'You do know I'm going to squish you all for this,' she roared.

The lieutenant smirked. 'And yet somehow you aren't.'

Lin slunk back. The tiny mite had a point. Lin met Fu's gaze across the cave. He whimpered as a battalion of ants charged at him, forcing him to curl up into a frightened panda ball.

Lin took a deep breath. She knew she would

be fine but she needed to rescue Fu. 'OK, OK,' she gave in. 'I'll leave the cameras if you promise to let us go.'

'Really?' the lieutenant suspiciously.

'Yes,' Lin nodded. 'I just wanted to get a message home to my brother and when the animal actors turned up, I thought they were going to steal my chance.'

'I spotted the animal actors too,' the lieutenant said. 'Some of my troops went out on a reconnaissance mission. They were all trodden on.' He dropped his head in remembrance of the fallen ants and the rest of his army joined him.

Lin saw her chance. 'So let's unite,' she said.

'We could turn **them** into sausages,' Fu agreed eagerly.

Ignoring Fu, Lin turned back to the mite. 'I was thinking it could be all of us against them!'

'And then what?' the lieutenant retorted. 'All the big animals get their time to shine on screen and we get nothing?'

'What do you mean? We are all equal at this

zoo.' Lin was confused.

'Some are more equal than others,' the lieutenant said. 'You big animals get all the attention, but nobody is ever bothered about us.'

'That's not true!' Lin argued.

Silence descended upon the ant cave.

A black ant marched up to the microphone. He saluted the chief lieutenant, who stepped aside to let him speak.

'Permission to speak freely, Madam Panda?' the ant asked.

Lin shrugged her shoulders and nodded him on.

'Today, at thirteen hundred hours, a troop of ants were taking a much-needed lunch break. They were eating popcorn when one of the said big animals grabbed the popcorn and ate them in the process too.' He bowed his head. 'This type of behaviour is commonplace. We are not seen, and we are not respected.'

Before Lin could respond, another ant came up to speak.

'Last week, we lost an entire ant infantry

battalion to an elephant who wasn't looking where he was going,' the ant said. 'I sent a message to the whole zoo to attend a memorial for the fallen but none of you came.'

'I didn't get the message—' Lin started.

'Didn't get the message?' the chief lieutenant snapped. 'I delivered it to you personally.'

Lin's toes curled with shame as she remembered last week a little red mite had crawled up her back and whispered something in her ear. She'd swatted him away and carried on playing bamboo Jenga with Fu.

Lin was glad her ears were covered in black fur so no one could see the deep red they had turned.

'You lot couldn't care less about us insects in this zoo,' the chief lieutenant continued. 'Every single ant here has their own story of being overlooked and partially stomped on.'

'That can't be true!' Lin turned to an ant by her shoulder. 'We don't treat you that badly, do we?'

The ant crawled down Lin's leg and marched over to the microphone. 'I can confirm that it is true, ma'am. We are thought of as lesser animals. We are the troops on the ground and in the trenches, making sure that the soil is fertilised and random lumps of sugar are eaten. Our work is unappreciated but if we stopped, you **would** feel the effects.'

Lin thought about every time she had seen a trail of ants marching bits of leaves on the uneven kerbs by the zoo path. She had never thought about it before but realised now that their work meant that vital plants were recycled so that **all** the animals could enjoy luscious pastures and plants the whole year round, including delicious bamboo.

'**Our** story never gets told,' the chief lieutenant said. 'Because the whole world prefers to listen to **your** story. When it comes to size, you big animals win every time. How can an ant compete with a fluffy panda?'

Lin found it hard to swallow with the lump in her throat. She'd thought that in making the zoo a place that prioritised animals over humans, all the animals and insects were happier. As she heard the ants speak of the times when they didn't feel as valued as the other animals, her shoulders curled in and her chin trembled.

She realised what she had to do.

'You're right,' she said, after listening to each

and every tale. 'We all have stories we need to tell but right now your story needs to be told more than the others.'

The chief lieutenant jumped down from the ant pyramid and strode over to Lin. He gave the command for the pandas to be released and thousands of ants jumped into action to untie the cables around Lin's and Fu's paws.

'We'll work together?' the chief lieutenant said into the mic.

'We'll work together,' Lin agreed.

If you don't mind, Chief, I've always wanted to be a stand-up comedian and now we have a microphone I thought I'd have a go. All eyes on the large ant.
Why did the ant go to the supermarket?
I know, I know! The ant needed a plaster?
No. The ant needed deodorANT.

It turned out that pandas and ants, as smart as they were and as well as they worked together, could not understand how to use a camera, but they gave it a good go anyway.

Luckily, there was a human Lin knew who could help the ants.

9

Mites, Camera, Action!

'As the sun drops beyond the horizon and against a sky the colour of fire, one hundred ants return home from the trenches. Brothers in arms, they troop side by side, their chief lieutenant leading the fierce battle cry

acknowledging they were the lucky ones who got to live another day.'

Lin watched on the monitor as Avid kneeled close to the anthills, narrating their epic story. A long, robotic arm with the tiniest of cameras at one end zoomed in on the chief lieutenant and trailed him, slow-mo-ing his march so that every single pulsation through his muscles was captured as he power-walked back home. Lin marvelled at these extraordinary action heroes as Avid explained into the camera how the teeny-weeny insects could floor a wolf spider in seconds.

'Those ants are naturals on camera,' Liony whispered. 'I can't believe they haven't had any formal acting lessons.'

'It's impressive,' Lin agreed.

She'd watched the entire footage of the ants' tale. Their lives were a constant test of survival. They dodged the deadly crash of elephant feet and the earth-shattering impact of falling twigs and rainfall that created tsunamis in the cracks of the pavement. Every time Lin had carelessly littered the ground around her with broken bamboo stems and green-leaf spitballs, she now knew she may well have caused unprecedented seismic activity for the ants below.

But no more.

Lin promised she would take the time to notice **everyone**, no matter what their size. And to make sure everyone felt equally valued in their zoo family.

Lin and Fu continued to watch the ants have their moment to shine on screen.

'Are you upset about not getting a message home to your brother?' Fu whispered, concerned.

Lin shook her head. In fact, it was quite the opposite. She'd gathered all the animals at the zoo to watch the recording and support the ants. And since filming had started, Lin felt a lightness in her heart and had barely noticed that she'd been humming her happy panda tune the entire time. You know the one:

Hmmmm, hmmmm, hmm, hmmm, hmmmmmm,

hmmmm, hmmmmmm, hmmmmmm, hmmmmm,

hmmmmm, hmm, hmm, hmmm (go on – join in)

hmmmm, hmmm, hm, hmmmmmm, hmmmmmm,

ahhhhhh, AHHHHHHH!

Lin shrugged. 'It's OK. I'm sure Face-Like-A-Bag-Of-Potatoes knows I'm OK. And I'll find another way to contact him soon anyway.'

'Well, **I** would've played the role of an ant very differently,' Singa said as he joined Lin to watch the filming. 'But I suppose these amateurs are not bad,' he admitted reluctantly as they saw an entire army of ants and mites lift Avid into the air with their super-strength.

'It was good to see you,' Liony said, standing tall and puffing out his chest at his cousin. 'You should really be on your way though, Singa.'

'It was good to see you too, Liony,' Singa replied.

But somehow Lin could tell neither of them meant it.

'Madam Panda, please report for duty,' came a shout over the loudhailer.

The chief lieutenant had ordered the battalion of ants to create the formation of a paw that looked like it was beckoning Lin over to join them.

The chief scrambled up Lin's paw and towards her head. He burrowed into her ear.

'I think we have some space at the end of the movie for you to send your message to your brother, Madam Panda,' he said.

Lin's jaw fell open. She hadn't expected this. 'Are you sure?' she asked.

The formation of the ants below parted, coaxing Lin towards the camera.

Lin took a deep breath. She'd thought about this moment since she'd arrived at the zoo. She'd dreamed about what she would say to Face-Like-A-Bag-Of-Potatoes when she next had the chance, if she **ever** had the chance.

She thought about how much she missed him and how she wanted to tell him about all her adventures, about her best pal Fu and how she was now friends with a lion.

She wanted to tell her brother how sorry she was that she let him take the blame the time she broke Poh Poh's bamboo stick – the one that had been passed down through the generations from their great-great-great-grandpandas and had been a treasured family heirloom that she had destroyed after a game of hide-and-seek.

And she desperately wanted to tell him about how she'd managed to make toothpicks out of lolly sticks to reach the bits of bamboo that got stuck in the back of her teeth. She knew he suffered the same ailment when it came to eating wet bamboo.

There were just so many important things she needed to say to her brother.

Lin took another deep breath. The light on the camera flashed red. This was it. This was her moment. This was her chance to express all the feelings bottled up in her heart.

The chief lieutenant nodded her on, giving her the cue to have her moment.

Lin looked straight into the camera lens and said: 'All right, Face-Like-A-Bag-Of-Potatoes?'

And she then smiled, stepping away from the camera.

'Is that all you wanted to say?' Fu exclaimed. 'After everything? After almost getting into a fight with the animal actors and then getting abducted by ants, **that** was your message home?'

'Yup,' Lin said. 'It was a good one, wasn't it?'

The chief lieutenant crawled back down Lin's paw and towards the loudhailer. 'It's time for a shot of the family,' the mite ordered.

The tigers, penguins, llamas, lizards, raccoons, monkeys, elephants, capybara, vultures, snakes, pigeons and all that lived in the zoo crowded in behind the anthills.

The larger animals offered a paw and helped the smaller animals perch on the higher

branches above so they could be seen. And the smaller animals helped the ants up on to a raised platform where they would be centre stage.

'And here we have an example of the natural kingdom adapting to assist one another,' Avid Dattenburrow spoke into the microphone. 'A respect among animals and insects here at the zoo is highlighted by the way the mammals stepped back to allow the mites and ants to tell their story.'

Lin snuck in near the back with Liony and Fu

and the tigers, and the little red mite joined her on her shoulder.

'Welcome to the troop, Madam Panda,' he shouted in her ear.

Fu hugged Lin and Liony close as the animals shot their final scene.

'Well, now, isn't that something?' Avid Dattenburrow said in awe as the camerawomen shouted 'CUT'.